http://www.brindlebooks.co.uk

A Little Book of Strange Tales

By

Richard Hinchliffe

Brindle Books Ltd

Copyright © 2022 by Richard Hinchliffe

This edition published by
Brindle Books Ltd
Unit 3, Grange House
Grange Street
Wakefield
United Kingdom
WF2 8TF
Copyright © Brindle Books Ltd 2022

ISBN 978-1-7398648-3-5

All of the characters in this book are fictitious, and
any resemblance to actual persons, living or dead, is
purely coincidental.

Contents

Introduction

I've always loved short stories, especially the strange ones. I remember, as a child, being transfixed whilst watching 'The Outer Limits', 'The Twilight Zone', or the Hammer horror anthology movies.

As I grew older, the necessity of having to perform mundane work to earn my living meant that I could no longer spend my evenings in front of the television. As a result, I began to spend a portion of my free time dreaming up my own stories.

Thinking up your own tales gives you the opportunity to drift off and explore other dimensions. You can find yourself in all sorts of places; from a little diner on a deserted country road, as in 'The Last Bus', to the far reaches of space with the main protagonist of 'Where there's Hope'.

This little collection of stories explores all sorts of unusual places and the strange, sometimes sinister, events that unfold there.

I hope that you have as much fun reading these tales as I did writing them.

Richard Hinchliffe

The Summer of the Ant War

Robbie squinted against the bright July sun and noticed that the two soldiers at the head of the column had paused, sensing danger. Then he marvelled at their courage as, without waiting for their comrades, they charged forward to engage the enemy. Hopelessly outnumbered, with no chance of survival, they went into battle, antennae twitching, and hacked madly at their foes until they were overpowered, dismembered and devoured.

Not wishing to see the carnage continue Robbie took a book from his satchel and stood it between the warring factions. The ants, confronted with the unknown, stopped. The forward scouts turned, perhaps in fear, or confusion, or perhaps simply seeking further orders, but the break in hostilities did not last very long. After a moment of chaos, the insects advanced upon each other again. Some moved around the book, some attempted to climb it. Both sides had the same goal: Destroy the enemy for the good of the colony.

Robbie hadn't noticed his father appear behind him.

"Ants, eh?" he muttered, looking over the boy's shoulder. "I'm sure I've got something in the shed for ants."

Robbie watched him march purposefully down the garden and wondered what his father could possibly have that the ants might want.

Presently, he returned with a brass spray can. He gently shooed the boy away before pumping the handle several times and spraying the entire battlefield with the contents of the can.

As the mist cleared, Robbie edged gingerly forward to see the resulting carnage. The ants were no longer fighting. A few were trying desperately to cling to life, staggering around aimlessly. It was a futile struggle, and within seconds they joined their fallen comrades and foes, the black and the red lying together, warriors at last united, awaiting ant Valhalla.

Robbie turned to ask his father why, but he was already walking away, returning the weapon to its resting-place. Perhaps, thought the boy, this little taste of Armageddon had been a warning to the ant colonies not to make war here. The deaths of these soldiers must have been the price of peace. That must be it, he decided, because adults were wise.

By the end of the summer, however, his father had systematically slaughtered every ant in the garden…

*   *   *

The blast woke him, hurling him the width of the trench. At first, he curled up, panic-stricken, into a foetal position. He was sure that he had been hit. After a moment, however, he realised that the pain in his head was due to the noise of the explosion, and the wetness that soaked through his trench coat was the mud, thrown up by the blast, half covering him. Still, he remained, a ball of quaking flesh and bone, unable to move or to speak.

"Snap out of it, Private!" someone barked, but he found that he could not respond.

"He's losing it, Sarge," a voice muttered. "He's in shock."

"Get him out of there," the first voice ordered.

Robbie distantly sensed hands grabbing him by the collar, dragging him from beneath the cold mud. A moment later he sat, shivering, a damp blanket wrapped tightly about him.

Someone had found his steel helmet and put it on his head, but he was vaguely aware, and strangely worried that he did not know where his weapon was – as if it would do him any good here.

"Private Thompson," the Sergeant growled, "pull yourself together!"

Unready to answer, he stared ahead, rocking gently back and forth in silence.

"Somebody sort this man out," said the sergeant, failing to hide his disgust as he waded away through the mud.

One of the other soldiers had found Robbie's rifle; the long bayonet already fixed, and placed it gently in his hands.

"Come on, Robbie," he said. "It'll be alright."

He sounded terrified and Robbie wondered whom he was trying to convince.

Time had passed – he didn't know how much – but it was dark now, and quiet, save for the occasional burst of a consumptive coughing fit and the distant moans of the wounded and the dying. There was a faint odour of tobacco smoke in the air. Some lucky bastard still had cigarettes.

Robbie wasn't totally sure if he was alright now, but he was able to look around him. Peering into the gloom, he could make out the silhouettes of the nearest men. They were huddled in silence; the collars of their trench coats turned up, hiding their features. Some of them shivered beneath filthy blankets, but all of them clutched their rifles, bayonets pointing skywards.

Presently, the sergeant paddled through the mud and paused, looking at Robbie.

"Private Thompson," he whispered.

"Yes, sergeant," Robbie said. Mercifully, his voice did not break.

The sergeant nodded, and now Robbie sensed no disapproval from the man. He was sure, in fact, that the expression on the rough face before him was one of compassion. He moved on in silence, checking each of the men under his command, perhaps torturing himself with silent farewells.

When the order came to go over the top, Robbie surprised himself by being one of the first up the makeshift ladder, but as he reached the top, the earth gave way and he fell back down into the trench. His rifle slipped back down after him, bayonet first, sticking into his thigh and tearing flesh. Unaware of the pain, or of the blood pouring down his leg, he picked up the weapon and clambered back up the ladder and onto the field. He tried to run forward but his feet sank into the mud until it reached his calves. Undaunted, he carried on as quickly as he could.

The Germans at the other end of the battlefield could not yet see the advancing soldiers, but were alerted by the officer's whistles and the battle cries of the men.

The machine guns started firing, chopping down bodies like a scythe through corn. The battle cries began to change to screams of pain and panic.

All about them the bullets whined past with a sound like giant mosquitoes. Robbie heard a loud crack as one of the deadly projectiles cut through the air much closer. He did not hear the next bullet, but felt a huge impact in his chest which, oddly, made him think of a time, years before, when he had seen a man kicked by a horse.

He lay on his back in the cold, stinking mud, his own heartbeat sounding deafeningly loud as he stared up at the sky. As his vision faded, he wondered if anyone else had noticed the huge airship overhead. It glowed like the moon.

"Strange," he thought, absently. "I've never seen one do that before," …and then it vanished as the black night engulfed him.

When he awoke, Robbie Thompson found himself in a white room, strapped to a white table. Although it looked like no room that he had ever seen before, he assumed that it was an operating theatre. That must be it, he reasoned. He had been picked up off the battlefield and brought to a hospital.

The sigh of relief had not left his lips before he noticed the figure in the room. At first glance, it appeared to be a child in a strange mask. As it moved closer, however, it became clear that it was not a mask.

In stark terror, Robbie recoiled, but only as far as the restraints about his limbs would let him. He was helpless. He tried to scream, but was able to make no sound. By now, he was much more terrified than he had been in the freezing, muddy trench, when death could have come at any moment.

The monster looked at him with its huge black eyes. There was no possibility of an expression in the grey, insect-like face. Its mouth was little more than a horizontal slit and the nostrils simply small triangular holes in an otherwise featureless expanse of leathery, grey skin. It moved forward, presenting what looked like a watch lens, and placed it on Robbie's forehead.

He heard a voice inside his head, or perhaps he just felt it, as he would have been unable to describe what it sounded like.

You are in no immediate danger, it said.

Incredibly…instinctively?…he knew how to answer, using his mind. He knew that the thing on his forehead was translating the creature's thoughts into phrases that he could understand.

"Where am I?" he asked.

You are on our airship. We have repaired your body and we are ready to begin tests.

"No…No, I want to go home," he said, his entire body shaking with panic.

You cannot go home, it replied. *It will take several human lifetimes for us to get to my home planet and several more to return here to yours.*

"Why?" Robbie stammered. "Why have you got to go…and come back?"

There was a pause before the creature replied. *Because I'm sure I've got something in the shed for humans*, it said.

Beady Eye

I am a beady eye.

I never close to sleep.

My surface glistens moistly,

But I shall never weep.

I am a beady eye,

And all I do is see,

But whilst I'm busy watching you,

Is someone watching me?

I am a beady eye,

And never have I cried,

Since I was pickled in this jar,

The night my owner died.

Siren Song

"Geri DeWinter was hard to control," said Benjamin Stone. "Did I say 'hard'? No. Geri DeWinter was impossible to control!" he continued, chuckling breathlessly. He seemed to grow ever more mirthful, until the laughter metamorphosed into a bout of coughing. When it finally subsided, he leaned forward and stubbed out his cigar in the ornate bowl on the coffee table, which served as an ashtray.

It had been like this for the last half-hour. Benjamin had happily answered every question that was put to him. He was enjoying the chance to talk to us and taking pleasure in the fact that we were so obviously entertained by his stories.

I looked across at Stacey as she checked that the little cassette recorder was still rolling. She noticed and flashed me her million-dollar smile.

"Marty, would you like to get some shots of Mr. Stone?" she asked.

"Sure," I said, attaching the flashgun to my camera.

As I raised the camera and centred Benjamin's huge, brown, smiling face in the viewfinder; I noticed a dark shape that seemed to loom behind him. Something smeared on the lens, I thought. I brought the camera down and suddenly the hairs on the back of my neck stood out. I was looking straight at Benjamin, but the shape was still there behind him. I glanced at Stacey, but she was checking her tape-counter. When I looked back at Benjamin, the shape was gone.

"You okay, son?" he asked.

"Yeah, I'm fine," I said, rubbing my eyes. "I'm just a little tired. It's been a long drive down."

There was a shuffling footstep in the hallway and the heavy door to the room creaked open, as if by itself.

After a couple of seconds, Clara appeared in the doorway, slowly edging her way into the room. She looked as though her frail and ancient body might give way under the weight of the tray she held. She eased the tray down onto the table and looked at each of us with her disapproving glare before setting out the bone china cups and saucers with the slow precision of a surgeon.

The rest of us sat perfectly still and silent. It was as if, when Clara entered the room, she sucked all the life and animation out of its occupants.

Sensing our discomfort, Benjamin broke the silence. "It's alright, Clara," he said. "I'll pour the tea."

She looked at him bitterly. For a moment I thought she was about to protest but she slowly turned and left the room, closing the door gently behind her. We waited, no one knowing what to say, until Benjamin leaned forward and began pouring out the tea.

"It's no secret," he said at last. "Clara and Geri barely spoke to each other in those last few years. Towards the end, Geri wouldn't even stay in the same room as Clara."

"But she continued to let Clara live here in her house?" said Stacey, switching the tape-recorder back on.

"She didn't have a choice," he replied simply. "Clara's my wife."

Stacey pressed on, obviously scenting that she was arriving at the real meat of the interview, rather than just humorous anecdotes.

"You must have meant an awful lot to Geraldine DeWinter, Mr. Stone," she said. "After all, she left you everything."

Benjamin looked at her for a long moment with great intensity. It was as if he was trying to read her mind.

Suddenly, his features softened, and the smile started widening on his huge face.

"She certainly did, Miss Harrison," he said. "You see, for most of her life, Geri DeWinter had nobody. Her Daddy ran off when she was a baby and her mother died young. At fourteen years old she just set off walking, moving north, getting whatever work she could find. It was somewhere 'round that time that she found her talent. She'd made her way to New Orleans. That's where she met Mamma Belle and she'd started singing."

Stacey was back on familiar ground now. She knew this part of the story.

"Yes. Mamma Belle was her mentor, wasn't she?" she asked. "She helped Geri to develop her voice?"

Benjamin's chuckle began again; growing stronger and stronger until it took control of his whole body. Eventually, as before, the laugh collapsed into a fit of coughing and wheezing. "Yeah, she helped Geri develop her voice," he said, between gasps, "but not in the way you think."

"She had some unorthodox coaching methods?" asked Stacey.

The combination of mirth and breathlessness got the better of him, and it was two or more minutes before he could answer.

"Oh yeah, you could say they were unorthodox methods," he chuckled, "if you think that Voodoo is unorthodox."

Stacey and I looked at one another. Was he kidding? We'd both heard the tales about Mamma Belle being some kind of Voodoo priestess but had, of course, dismissed them as stupid stories. Was Benjamin Stone simply perpetuating the old myth to add some mystique to the story of Geri DeWinter?

Stacey was smiling now, half-expecting Benjamin to throw a punch line to the joke, and quite happy to feed him.

"Are you telling us, Mr. Stone, that Mamma Belle used Voodoo to give Geri DeWinter her talent?"

His eyes widened in a comical expression of incredulity. "Give her talent?" he said. "No," he beamed his big smile again, "but she used it to preserve that talent."

I lined up my camera and took three shots of Benjamin. Each time the camera flashed, comically late, he would face me and widen his smile. I got the impression that he was playing with Stacey, letting her curiosity build whilst he performed his little comedy routine.

His game was obviously working. Stacey threw me a frosty glare. Reluctantly, I lowered the camera and smiled broadly at Benjamin, feeling happy to have been allowed to play.

"So, Mr. Stone," said Stacey. "Mamma Belle was a what? A Voodoo high priestess?"

"Guess so," he replied. "I never took much heed of that sort of thing."

"So whatever supposed magic she used didn't actually have any effect on Geri DeWinter, did it?" Stacey said. She had been put out by Benjamin's little game, but she seemed reasonably happy now that she felt he was just throwing in some background colour to the story.

"All I know about it," said Benjamin, suddenly serious, "is that Geri DeWinter could go out and perform fourteen shows a week. In between that, she could drink more hard liquor and smoke more cigarettes than I could. Not once did her voice ever show the slightest sign of it."

His gaze became a little more distant and his voice soft and low as he remembered. He seemed almost unaware of our presence. "Every time that woman opened her mouth," he continued, "she made a sound prettier than all the angels in Heaven. Just hearing her voice would make you fall in love with her."

I could see that his eyes were moist with tears. It was obvious that he had felt intense emotion for Geri DeWinter, and I was beginning to understand the rift between her and Clara Stone.

"Did you fall in love with Geri DeWinter, Mr. Stone?" asked Stacey.

I looked at her, open-mouthed, hardly believing that she had dared to ask. Benjamin, however, took it in his stride.

"I loved Geri DeWinter, Miss Harrison," he said, "but when I married Clara, many, many years ago, I took vows. I never once broke those vows, and I never would. Clara understood that, and Geri came to understand it too."

"When you say that Geri 'came to understand,' does that mean that she took some convincing?" asked Stacey.

He shrugged. "Not from me," he continued. "Mamma Belle was the one that convinced her that wedding vows shouldn't be broken. She never argued, and we became best friends."

I was relieved that Stacey had decided to leave that line of questioning. Whilst this tale of unrequited love would add even more poignancy to the tale of Geri DeWinter, I was glad that she didn't want to dwell on the bitterness that it must have caused between Geri and Clara.

"There is something else that I'd like to ask you about," said Stacey, "and I know that you've been reluctant to talk about it in the past."

"I knew you would," said Benjamin. "Everybody that comes here asks about it. You mean the last recording."

"That's the one," Stacey smiled. "It's rumoured to be the best thing she ever did. They say she poured her entire soul into that last song."

Benjamin nodded slowly. "Yes, Miss Harrison," he confirmed. "They do say so."

Suddenly, the door creaked open, and Clara hobbled over the threshold. "Benjamin," she said. "It's time for your medicine."

He sighed, like a man whose patience is wearing very thin, then sat back in resignation. "Alright, Clara," he said, "I'll be right there."

He struggled up onto his feet. "Excuse me," he said to us. "This won't take too long. It doesn't do a damned bit of good, but I've learned it's easier just to take it than to fight Clara about it."

When Benjamin left the room, Stacey poured herself another cup of tea. "I think he's going to tell us about it," she said, excitedly.

"He didn't say that he would," I pointed out.

"He didn't say that he wouldn't," she countered. "You never know: He might even let us hear it!"

"I doubt it," I said. "You can bet that Clara wouldn't let us hear it, no matter what he said."

Stacey was deep in thought. "I wonder where they keep it?" she pondered.

From the bowels of the big house came the sound of Benjamin, coughing and retching.

"My God, he sounds terrible," said Stacey.

"Well," I replied, "they told us before we set off that he was ill. To be honest, I don't think the guy has long left."

"No," said Stacey, "and neither do we."

"What do you mean?" I asked, though I began to feel an icy apprehension as I caught the look on her face.

"I've got to hear that song," she said simply, picking up her cassette recorder and making for the door. "If Benjamin comes back before me, just tell him I had to use the bathroom."

She pulled the door open with a loud creaking sound and, before I could form any words to stop her, she vanished out of the door.

I stood in silence for a moment, worrying about consequences. What the Hell did Stacey think she was playing at? How could she go sneaking about like that in someone else's house? This was bad, I thought, very bad.

I heard the shuffle of Clara's footsteps outside the room and her head peered around the door. In the space of about a second, her expression changed from its usual look of stern disapproval to one of shock and fear as her eyes widened. I tried to appear as relaxed as I could manage.

"Stacey's just gone to use the bathroom," I said, busily fiddling with my camera to hide my discomfort.

Just then, I heard it: From somewhere upstairs came the faint, muffled sound of music, the strings, the horns, and then a woman's voice. I couldn't make out the words, but there was something utterly mesmerising in the sound of the voice…

Clara's mouth fell open and she took in a sharp breath, as if she was going to scream. Instead, she shouted. "Benjamin," she bellowed, "she's playing it!" There was wild panic in her voice. She turned away and I heard her shuffling footsteps getting faster, then the creak of the stairs as she ascended.

I moved slowly towards the door with a sick feeling in my stomach, not knowing how we were going to explain this. Stacey would have to do all the talking, I decided. This had nothing to do with me, and I would make that clear.

I heard Benjamin hobbling through the house, gasping and panting as he rushed as fast as he could. As I came out of the room he appeared in front of me, his face a mask of blind panic.

"What in God's name has she done?" he gasped. He looked towards the top of the big, polished wood staircase and my gaze followed his. The music had stopped. Now, there were two voices, both raised in fury. One of the voices was Clara's; the other I didn't recognise.

"I knew he should have got rid of it," shouted Clara.

"Oh, you'd have liked that wouldn't you, Missy?" replied the other voice. "Well, Honey, it's too late for you now. I ain't takin' no more of your shit! You done, baby!"

There was a sound; a sickening wet thud and then a horrendous, high pitched wail of pain and shock. Clara appeared at the top of the stairs, gripping the banister rail in an effort to retain her balance. A dark river of blood poured down her bony face from her hairline. She fell forwards down the stairs, her frail limbs swinging this way and that as she tumbled over and over until she lay, twisted and lifeless, at the bottom of the stairs. The pool of blood under her head grew around her and her sightless, dead eyes looked straight at me.

"Jesus, no!" said Benjamin, and his gaze slowly lifted back to the top of the stairs. There, in the half shadow of the landing, stood Stacey, a horrifying, fixed smile on her blood-splattered face. In her raised hand she held a heavy brass candlestick. She held it upside down and one corner of its solid, square base was thickly stained with blood. She looked down with glassy eyes and the strange smile widened when her empty gaze fell on Benjamin. When she spoke, it wasn't with her own voice. "Benjamin, honey," she said, "I have missed you so much. Now don't you worry, Darlin'. We together again now, for always."

Time Ended

The Astronaut, who a moment before had been floating, was suddenly dragged into the black hole's gravity well. He became one with the black hole's mass. Time ended…

Then suddenly, it began again…

He was on a beach. The cries of gulls drifted on the wind, carried off in a dying echo. The sun was dazzlingly bright, though the sky that day was of a rich blue, stark against the white clouds on the horizon.

The huge ocean swelled like the movements of a living, breathing thing, so unpredictable, so powerful. He curled his toes against the wet sand as the ocean's edge reached out and touched his feet. The moment was frozen in time.

A voice, in his head, in his whole being, spoke to him. "This is you?" it asked.

He thought at first that he must be going mad, but realised that the voice was coming from somewhere else. He was communicating with another entity, somewhere inside the black hole. It was impossible... but it was happening.

"This is you?" it asked again, this time with a shadow of impatience.

"Yes" he replied, "this was me as a child."

"Ocean beast is a major living entity on your planet?"

He thought about the question, at first about to explain that the ocean was not considered a living entity, but then he decided not to. He had thought of it that way himself, seconds before in another existence.

"Yes," he replied, "a major living entity."

He uncurled his toes in the shallows as if to reach out himself. He became a part of the ocean, a part of the world, the universe, everything. The moment was frozen in time.

"You were one?" asked the entity.

"Yes," he replied, "I think so."

"You think so?"

He stepped forward into the ocean, deeper and deeper. His mother looked up from her book, flicked back a strand of her long black hair, a look of concern growing in her dark eyes. She got to her feet, a lithe, bronzed figure in a blue, one-piece bathing costume. She shouted his name, but her voice was lost on the wind, replaced by the cries of the gulls.

The sea was at his chest, the currents pushing and pulling at him, threatening to throw him off balance with each step. One minor swell took his head beneath the surface and with one step forward he was in another environment.

The panic was sudden. It came with the realisation that the air in his lungs was running out. He had to resist the body's natural urge to breathe in and, stricken with terror for his life, he tried to turn and head for the shore. He tripped, lost his balance as the currents pulled him down. He could hold his breath no longer. He inhaled, then wretched as the ocean reached into his lungs. He thrashed his limbs wildly, totally unaware of which direction he was facing, all hope gradually abandoned as his body was thrown into convulsions by the liquid invading him, cutting off vital supplies of oxygen to the organs of his body. Like a retreating army, his thoughts abandoned what they could no longer control: The outside world; the ocean around him; his limbs; his internal organs; his brain; him. The moment was frozen in time.

"You were fearful of becoming one?" asked the entity.

"Yes," he said, feeling the terror of the moment. "I was fearful."

He began to black out, the stark reality of the moment only even happening to him now in thin slices of seemingly disconnected time. Events with no meaning now that he knew that death was imminent.

"Can you feel yourself becoming one?" It was the voice of the entity, but it was here in his childhood.

"Yes," he said. "You were here as well, weren't you? Long before I fell into the black hole."
"I have always been here," said the entity. "Here, there is only the now. No future, no past."

Hands were pressed into his back and a solution of ocean and bile ejected from his lungs; the taste acrid. His body dragged air inside with a tortured rasp. Three minutes of agony ensued as the same body desperately, gratefully readjusted to being alive. The hands that had pushed the invading ocean back out of him now held him, their brown arms wrapped around him for protection. He looked up at the dark eyed woman who had saved him, but his child brain had no way to adequately express his gratitude.

"The moment is frozen in time," she said, but he was not puzzled by his mother's use of the phrase. It was as if he had heard it before, somewhere, or always known it.

She carried him back to the wooden, beach -front house and put him to bed. She left his bedroom door open so that she could keep watch over him after his ordeal. He was vaguely aware of her setting up her easel in the main room. She would be painting sunsets by candlelight, he thought absently; standing with the handle of her brush tapping lightly on her perfect white teeth as she stared out of the huge windows, to the sky. She often stood for hours like that, lost in her own lonely thoughts.

He sank gratefully and contentedly to sleep. The smell of the fresh, clean sheets on his bed seeming to relax him further. The dark eyed woman turned from her view of the sky and looked back at her child. She saw the steady, even breathing of good, healthy sleep and smiled.

She pulled the bedroom door so that it was almost closed and opened the lid of an ancient portable record player. She ran a finger along a shelf full of records and selected one; Cassandra Wilson singing Tupelo Honey. She turned the volume down so as not to disturb the sleeping boy, then went to the kitchen, which was divided from the main room by only a breakfast bar made of driftwood with a metal worktop. From a drawer she took out a bottle of pills, took two and returned the bottle. The label read: Dothiapin, 100mg. Two tablets to be taken a day. Avoid alcohol.

She shrugged and fixed herself a scotch and lemonade, with ice from the antique refrigerator that buzzed and rattled intermittently in the corner. With the scotch at her elbow, the log fire crackling and the music barely audible from the record players tiny, built in speaker, she sat cross-legged on the huge, overstuffed sofa and pulled the coffee table towards her. In the middle of it was a wooden box. She opened it and took out a cigarette, lit, inhaled and held a breath before letting the used smoke out in a thin, blue-grey stream.

In the distance, the water's edge lapped the shore, sparkling here and there with the reflection of the rising moon. To her, it felt as if the ocean was waiting like a spider in a web, knowing that prey was plentiful.

The same ocean that had claimed her husband's life three years ago had today almost claimed her child, but she could not leave. She refused to fear the ocean, or hate it, just as she hoped that her son would refuse. She would speak with him later, she decided, and find out about his feelings towards it.

"What does the ocean mean to you?" she asked him one evening as they sat on the porch, her with her arms around him, guarding him from the outside world.

He narrowed his eyes and looked out to the sea. "It's Daddy," he said, sure that his father had now become part of the living ocean.

She kissed his hair and felt a tear form in her eye. "Yes, it is," she said, and realised why she could never leave.

*   *   *

His mother was out working, and he had the beach house, and the beach, to himself. No one ever came here. "It's too far off the beaten track," his mother would often say before adding. "It's Nowheresville, that's why it's safe."

With the extra money that she made working in a local diner, she had bought him a television set to keep him company while she was out working.

He thought about that, and his child mind accepted the logic as he watched a television show about the history of space travel, in which astronauts walked on the moon in flickering monochrome.

He ate his supper of biscuits and milk, and drifted peacefully to sleep. In the background, at the edge of his consciousness, the television played on. The sounds of Mission Control were the last sounds that he heard as he reached the edge and was dragged over...

...Dragged over what? For a moment he couldn't remember...

...And then it all came back to him. He breathed out and listened to the strange echo inside his space helmet. Just there, on the other side of his visor, was an environment so alien, so hostile, that exposure to it by any damage to the EVA suit would result in certain, instantaneous death. On previous missions, the thought had terrified him, on this one it was an irrelevance. Despite what the theorists had told him, he was a logical man, and he knew that strapping on a jet-pack and falling into a black hole would certainly result in his body being torn into string then crushed by forces unimaginable by the human mind…And still he had volunteered. He knew that he didn't get picked for this assignment because he was the best volunteer, he was picked because he was the only volunteer, the only astronaut dumb enough…and he was scared.

"Mishcon, this is Lemming one. What's my status?" he asked shakily.

"Hermes one, this is Mishcon. Please use your correct designation. Your status is A-okay. T – minus three minutes," his headphones replied.

"Mishcon," he said to the disembodied voice in his spacesuit. "I'm about as far from civilisation as it gets. I'm just about to fall into a black hole for you people. I'll choose my own designation. Lemming one, out!"

There was a long pause, then: "Hermes one, this is Mishcon. Please respond."

No...no way, no how. I'm jumping into a black hole, about to be totally annihilated by cosmic forces and I can't even choose my own designation.

"Hermes one, this is Mishcon," the voice said, now with a sort of tired patience. "According to all the readings we're getting, you seem to be suffering a major anxiety attack. Please respond."

"OF COURSE I'M GETTING A MAJOR FUCKING ANXIETY ATTACK," he screamed, "I'M JUMPING INTO A FUCKING BLACK HOLE!"

"Hermes one, this is Mishcon," the voice came back. "Try the relaxation techniques you were taught. Don't worry. We anticipated for some anxiety on a mission like this."

"No shit, Sherlock," said the astronaut.

Something bleeped…

"What the fuck was that?" he asked. "Mishcon, what was that bleep?"

"Calm down, Hermes One," the voice answered. "You know what it was. Thirty seconds to event horizon."

"Christ! Already?" He began to feel the panic rise in his chest. What in God's name was he doing here? He wasn't just getting old and dying like a normal human being, he was being thrown through the gates of Hell just so that they could measure the results. He wanted to scream, to run…

…He didn't. He checked the control panel on his left arm…his left arm…The bastards had even given him a right – handed spacesuit.

"Give me countdown, Mishcon," he said, soberly.

"Roger that, Lemming One," said the voice. "Good luck. T – minus ten seconds, nine, eight, seven….siix…..fiiive……fooooouuuuuur………..thr

eeeeeeeeeeeeeeeeeeee………………….twooooooooooo
oooooooooooooooooooooooooooooooooooooooooooo."
There was a strange, sickening lurch as the spaceman felt himself being pulled over the edge, though it was perceptible in no other way. The ultimate loss of control of one's own existence…

…falling….

Falling from where? He couldn't remember. And then the harsh crack of his head on the bare wooden floor of the beach house knocked him conscious. He had fallen off the sofa.

Mother was home now. Seeing that he wasn't hurt, just vaguely bewildered as he often was when coming out of a dream, she smiled.

"Good morning, baby," she said.

"I'm not a baby," he replied sullenly.

"You're my baby."

"I'm grown up now," he said, and believed it.

"Even when you're a spaceman, you'll still be my baby," she said.

They ate breakfast together and laughed a lot, then afterwards, they painted pictures with a watercolour set that she had bought them.

"Why do you enjoy painting?" she asked, always happy to hear her child's opinions and ideas.

He looked at his own painting, a crude representation of the world he knew, and felt, for an instant, frozen in time. And it felt good. He smiled at her but said nothing.

Mother smiled back. "That's the best reason of all," she said.

Towards the bottom of the picture was his impression of a large white rock, like one that he had found recently on the beach. His eyes fell upon, then focussed upon it...a patch of white so empty...so perfect...The whiteness seemed to draw him further in...

"Beyond the light barrier, Mishcon," he said. "Who knows, someone might hear this message in a million years' time." Deep down, of course, he knew rationally that his transmission would never escape the event horizon. Nothing ever did.

The vastness overwhelmed him.....The living presence overwhelmed him.....

"Who are you?" he asked.

"We are one" replied the entity. "The instant that you fall into the black hole, time ends for you. You have always been here, and you always will be."

Suddenly, all physical sensation left him. He could not feel the spacesuit or any part of his body. The distinction between himself and the entity vanished.

He searched, panic – stricken, for some part of his humanity within his mind.

"My memories," he gasped, "they're part of me, part of my *life history.*"

But the only reply came from within him, from the infinite thing that he was. They were not memories, simply alternate possibilities. If time did not exist, then there had been no past. If time did not exist, he reasoned, then he could never have been an astronaut, just a singularity that dreamed it was a man."

The Unhappy Courtship

We've been together fifteen days,

Already, dear, it's Hell.

You know I hate to ask you this,

But did you know you smell?

And tell me, are you sleeping well?

Oh please, don't tell me lies,

It's obvious, my dear,

From those black rings around your eyes.

I've never courted anyone

Quite like you before.

In sleep your mouth hangs open

But I never hear you snore,

Except the night that you sat up

And let out one deep breath.

I must confess, when you did that

It scared me half to death.

And this nightgown of snowy white

Doesn't look too good on you

But on the wage I'm paid for scrubbing slabs

Well, what am I to do?

I may leave you yet for someone else,

For you're no fragrant rose,

And tell me dear, why do you wear

That tag upon your toes?

Time Continued

The Astronaut, who a moment ago had been floating, was suddenly dragged towards the black hole's gravity well. Soon, he would become one with its mass. He was sure that time would end, and to all intents and purposed, he would be lost forever, crushed into a point singularity where the laws of the universe simply did not exist.

He tensed, closed his eyes and expected the worst. He was more terrified than he had ever been…and then, just as he became convinced that everything was going wrong, he heard the bleep of his helmet speaker.

Offering a silent prayer, he forced his eyes open. The sight that greeted him caused him to release an almost orgasmic sigh of relief. The incredible cascade of brilliant colours indicated that the planned gateway was opening within the black hole.

Time continued. The jetpack strapped to his back adjusted his rate of fall, sending him toward the growing ball of brilliant light at the centre of the swirling kaleidoscope. The terror of the awesome journey gripped him.

"This is bound to go wrong," he thought. "I must be fucking crazy!"
"Mishcon, this is Lemming one. What's my status?" he asked shakily.

"Hermes one, this is Mishcon. Please use your correct designation. Your status is A-okay. T-minus three minutes," his headphone replied.
"Mishcon," he said to the disembodied voice in his spacesuit, "I'm about as far from civilisation as it gets. I'm just about to fall into a black hole for you people. I'll choose my own designation. Lemming one, Out!"

There was a long pause, then: "Hermes one, this is Mishcon. Please respond."

No…No way, no how. I'm jumping into a black hole, about to be totally annihilated by cosmic forces and I can't even choose my own designation.

"Hermes one, this is Mishcon," the voice said, now with a sort of tired patience. "According to all the readings we're getting, you seem to be suffering a major anxiety attack. Please respond."

"OF COURSE I'M SUFFERING A MAJOR ANXIETY ATTACK," he screamed, "I'M JUMPING INTO A FUCKING BLACK HOLE!"

"Hermes one, this is Mishcon," the voice came back. "Try to use the relaxation techniques you were taught. Don't worry. We anticipated for some anxiety on a mission like this."

"No shit, Sherlock," said the astronaut.

Something bleeped…

"What the fuck was that?" he asked. "Mishcon, what was that bleep?"

"Calm down, Hermes one," the voice answered. "You know what it was. Thirty seconds to event horizon."

"Christ! Already?"

He began to feel the panic rise in his chest. What in God's name was he doing here? He wasn't just getting old and dying like a normal human being; he was being thrown through the gates of Hell just so that they could test some screwball theory about faster-than-light travel. He wanted to scream, to run away…

…He didn't. He checked the control panel on his left arm…his *left* arm!…The bastards had given him a right-handed spacesuit.

"Give me countdown, Mishcon," he said soberly.

"Roger that, Lemming one," said the voice. "Good luck! T-minus ten seconds, nine, eight, seven…siix….fiiiiive……..foooouuuur…..thrrrrreeee eeeeeeee…twooooooooooooooooooooooooo….."

There was a strange, sickening lurch as the spaceman felt himself being pulled over the edge, though it was perceptible in no other way. The ultimate loss of control of one's own existence…falling…

…The light grew brighter as he fell towards it, until it was almost unbearable. He felt the control panel on his arm, found the button to operate his outer visor, and pressed. Silently, a thin, green film slid over the front of his helmet, shielding his stinging eyes from the incredible luminosity. He felt the tears running down his cheeks as he blinked, trying to regain his vision.

The gravitational forces of the gateway pulled at him, hurled him blindly around like an insect down a waste pipe. He felt his stomach churn. No amount of tests or training could have prepared him for this, he realised, dreading the feeling as his oesophagus went into the spasm of anti-peristalsis.

He retched, his empty stomach cramping as if to punish him, as he silently cursed the doctors at Mission Control, who had stopped him eating solids for the last twenty-four hours.

Finally, his body surrendered a mouthful of bitter, acidic bile which splattered against his visor before splashing back into his face.

At last, the eddying of the cosmic whirlpool became too much, and consciousness was dragged from him, leaving only a total and unrelenting blackness…

…Suddenly, he was awake, floating in total darkness. Panic gnawed at him. Where was he? What had happened?

"Audio on," said an unfamiliar voice in his helmet speaker.

"Hello, Mishcon?" he asked, surprised…No reply.

An instant later, the stars appeared, as if from nowhere.

"What's going on?" he wondered.

"Visual on," said the strange voice.

"Mishcon," the astronaut asked. "What's going on? I was out cold. When I came around, I couldn't see."

"Hermes one," said the more familiar voice of the Mission Controller, "this is Mishcon. T-minus three minutes and counting."

It didn't make sense, he thought. He had already fallen into the black hole.

"Mishcon, this is Hermes one," he announced shakily. "What's happening? I've already been into the singularity. Why am I back here?"

"Hermes one, this is Mishcon," the voice replied. "As you know, some disorientation is natural. Please continue. T-minus two minutes thirty."

Something was wrong, he was sure of it.

"Mishcon," the astronaut said emphatically, "I am not suffering disorientation. I have already entered the singularity once. What the fuck is going on?"

A pause, and then: "Hermes one, this is Mishcon. Hold your position."

"You bet I'll hold my position. I'll hold my position until somebody tells me what the fuck is happening!"

There was no sound, save his ever more rapid breathing. He was about to speak again, to demand answers, but the speaker crackled to life once more…

"Hermes one, hold please," it said.
Faintly, he could hear the activity of Mission Control, the voices of unknown technicians shouting out

readings from their stations…and something else…a conversation:

"What's wrong this time Charlie?"

"It's the simulation. I don't get it. We're supposed to be running scenario eighty-seven-B, but the thing's developed a malfunction."

"Hello, Mishcon," said the astronaut. "Will somebody please tell me what's going on?"

He was ignored as the technicians continued their conversation:

"How long has the simulation been running?"

"Less than a minute. It's claiming that it's already completed the mission."

"It?" thought the astronaut. "Simulation?!" This time, he shouted: "What the fucking hell is going on, you bastards? Speak to me!!!"

"My God," said the helmet-speaker, and then: "Hello, Hermes one. Is that you?"

"Of course it's me! What's this crap about a simulation? Why am I back here? What's happening?"

When the Mission Controller replied, he sounded as confused and overwhelmed as the astronaut felt.

"Hermes one," he said. "I'm not sure exactly why this is happening, but we're experiencing an unusual malfunction with this simulation."

"What simulation?" the astronaut demanded. "What in Christ's name are you talking about?"

The voice from the speaker was replaced by another; colder, more authoritative.

"*You* are the simulation," it said.

"What the hell are you on about?" the spaceman spat through gritted teeth. "I'm Captain John Cooper. I demand to speak to the control Director!"

"Captain Cooper is dead," the voice said. "He has been dead for three months. You are a computer simulation, which incorporates some of Captain Cooper's brain patterns. Do you understand?"

This was complete Bullshit, Cooper thought.

Aloud, he said: "Is this some sort of joke?"

The cold voice continued to echo in his helmet, ignoring him, speaking to someone else at Mission Control. "I've heard of this happening before, but never seen it," it said. "Make sure that you erase the previous scenario from the hard drive completely when you start a new one."

"But what about *him*?" the Mission Controller asked.

"Him? It's not a *him*, it's an *it*. Just because the damn machine *thinks* that it's Captain Cooper doesn't mean that you have to humour it."

"Yeah, but… How much of Cooper's brain pattern was scanned into the computer? I mean, couldn't it be possible that this is….?"

"What? Cooper's soul? Grow up man! This project is costing over a trillion dollars an hour! Switch the God-damned thing off and start again!"

"Wait!" said Cooper. This couldn't be happening. He was alive. He knew it. He *felt* it. It was some kind of trick…surely…A test, he thought, to see how he reacted to stress. Yes, that must be it.

"Okay Guys," he said. "That's enough."

…and then there was nothing…
…Time ended…
…The astronaut, who a moment before had been floating, was suddenly dragged towards the black

hole's gravity well. A warning siren bleeped inside his helmet.

"Christ, NO!" he said, activating the jet-pack on his back and hoping, praying, that it wasn't too late to escape...

...It was. He screamed as he felt the crushing agony of his feet, then his legs, being dragged out into a long, thin rope of human tissue. Through the unbearable pain, he barely had time to beg the Almighty to get it over quickly.

Where There's Hope

Captain Sharpe looked out of the window of her stateroom at the stars and thought of home. How long had it been since she had last seen a blue sky, she wondered? Too long. She tried to remember what a gentle breeze felt like, or the smell of freshly mowed grass. The thought of returning to Iowa and re-living these half-forgotten experiences had been the main thing keeping her alive since the accident. Had it not been for the knowledge that she was on her way home, the months of lying immobile with only the view of the sifting stars would have driven her insane.

A buzzer sounded and she knew it was time for sleep. The medical unit connected to her body would release a tranquilliser into her bloodstream and in a few seconds she would rest. As her eyelids began to close, she wondered what dreams the computer would send through the system connected to her brain…

She opened her eyes and was immediately struck by the brightness. She was used to the stateroom being in darkness, save for the ambient light of the stars outside. What greeted her now, as she stared out of the window, left her breathless and awe-struck. An unspeakable joy consumed her as she gazed at the immense blue sphere of the Earth, filling the window, illuminating the stateroom with its magnificent radiance. She was home!

She was aware that the restraint field that had held her for the long months since the accident was not activated. With a monumental effort, she tensed aching muscles in an attempt to sit up, but was immediately aware of a firm but gentle hand pushing her back down.

She turned her head and felt a beautiful, joyful pain in the muscles of her neck. It was the first time in God knew how long that she had been able to move her head. A handsome young face was smiling down at her. It was a face that she had never seen before but it brought her such joy that she couldn't help smiling her warmest smile.

"Take it easy, Captain," said the young man, smiling back at her. "You've been immobile for a long time, and you've undergone major surgery in the last few months. I'm afraid I'm going to have to give you a thorough examination before you can move."

"Please," she said, "call me Ava."

The handsome young man smiled again. "Well, it's not protocol, but if you insist, Ava," he replied. "I'm Doctor Barclay, but you can call me Jim. Now, keep still."

She felt his strong, but gentle hands pressing against her stomach, her chest, her thighs. She knew that, to him, she was just another patient, that his examination was professional and efficient. And yet, as she let out a shaking exhalation of breath, she felt close to sheer ecstasy. It had been so long since she had felt the touch of another human being, let alone that of a handsome young man, that his cursory physical examination felt like the most beautiful, sensual thing that she had ever experienced.

She felt her cheeks flush as she lay, eyes closed with his hands upon her, and hoped that he didn't notice, lest he should somehow guess at the images in her mind.

He lifted his hands away and she slowly opened her eyes.

"You're in great shape," he said. "In fact, it's hard to believe you've been in the restraint field for more than a couple of weeks."

"It's been months," she said. "Three or four, maybe longer. What date is it?"

"Your injuries have healed perfectly," he said absently. As he did so, he rested a hand, very gently, on her thigh.

His touch immediately took her breath away. She felt the urgent, overpowering 'butterflies in the stomach' sensation and a weakness in her knees. Her breathing became quicker. She could not be mistaken, she was sure. He was as attracted to her as she was to him.

"Your medical computer's done an amazing job to keep you in such great condition." His eyes were smiling as he said it, hiding his complements behind a veneer of professionalism.

"Play it cool, Ava," she thought to herself. "Don't scare him off by acting like a bitch in heat."

"It's top of the range," she said, with a playful smile of her own. "It's the Uncle Mark Three, from the Wray Corporation. The cross-referencing sub-routines mean it can more-or-less think like a person. I guess it liked me enough to want to keep me alive, no matter what."

He was looking straight into her eyes now, no longer playful, no longer attempting to hide his attraction to her.

"I don't blame it," he said. He lifted his hand from her thigh and gently touched her cheek. "From now on," he continued, "I'm going to take care of you. I'm authorising your transport to the surface into my care. It'll take an hour or so to arrange a shuttle and then we'll be together. Sleep for a while."

He leaned forward and kissed her lips gently. She put an arm about his neck, returning the kiss with more passion before releasing him and lying back with a deep contented sigh.

"What a way to come home," she murmured as her eyes closed and she drifted to sleep...

The Uncle Mark Three calculated the readings from Captain Sharpe. The homecoming dream that it had created had returned her endorphin levels to within an acceptable state. The memories of the dream would have to be purged so that it could be re-used when needed. The clock-function in the medical unit would have to be re-set so that she would believe that only months had passed since her accident, and the restraint field would require recharging to ensure that she continues to look out of the window. If she were to move her head and see her own ancient and withered body, she might lose hope of ever seeing Earth and her health may suffer even more than it had in the forty years since the accident.

The Co-operative

Sofia looked down at the ketchup stain on her new, white, tight fitting T-shirt and quietly cursed. She had put it on that morning, along with the matching mini skirt and calf length boots with the express intention of turning heads and catching herself a young man. Now she would have to walk home to change, wasting at least two of the thirty-six hours of free time that she had left for the month.

She shrugged inwardly and continued her meal. Slumped in the red, moulded plastic seat, she took a big bite from her BigMac and chewed idly as she looked out of the huge window, past the golden arches, at Mecca.

She liked it here. It reminded her of the happy Friday mornings she had spent as a child with her grandfather:

He would sit, cloudy eyes staring into the distance, his shaking hands caressing the handle of his walking stick, as if trying to conjure up some half-remembered tactile impression of the AK47 assault rifle. As he sat, he would tell her tales of the old days, and the struggle:

About a hundred years ago, he had told her, the world had been run by a handful of business corporations. They had gradually taken control of each country's economy, and then their governments. At first, the majority of the population had been indifferent to this. After all, they had thought, cultural identity was no substitute for cheap goods. As the years went by, however, some people began to feel that individuals were becoming devalued that they had become a commodity, their only real purpose to create wealth for a handful of people running a handful of corporations.

Eventually, these dissenters began to organise into groups, to fight back against this all-powerful, global economic cartel. The first attempts at fighting back, small pockets of resistance were quickly crushed...but they were not wiped out entirely. Strangely, the ease with which these revolutionaries were defeated, the apparent futility of their struggle, won a widespread, if quietly voiced, sympathy for their cause. It was not long before more dissenters formed into groups and, as humans occasionally do when they perceive a common threat, however vague, the various groups put aside their differences and formed a co-operative. The stated aim, indeed the entire purpose, of this co-operative, was to take power from the corporations and give everyone a share of the benefits that had so far been enjoyed only by the corporation's owners. This had been the beginning of the last great global war, and of the new world order that had followed...

As she finished her burger and washed it down from the half-litre carton of Coca-Cola, Sofia wondered briefly what kind of world it would have been if the co-operative had lost the war. What kind of terrible responsibilities and choices would have been hers? As she walked out into the sunshine, she let the thought slip into a favoured daydream, in which she had been chosen as one of the organisers of the co-operative, running the big companies on behalf of the people, instead of manning the factories for them.

The Last Bus

The hitchhiker came in looking shook up. They usually do. He had that haunted look on his face that people get when they think that they've only just missed being killed by something…or someone.

He took a moment to get used to the dim lighting in the place, then sat on one of the high stools at the counter. It was only then that I let him know I'd noticed him by looking up from my newspaper.

"What can I get you?" I asked.
"Espresso." Looking at the price list on the wall behind me, he fished some change out of his pocket and slapped it on the counter.

I went to my pre-historic Espresso machine and did one of the things I do best, whilst sneakily glancing over at my only other customer, who was doing her best not to notice anything. She was studying the ten item menu from the table as if it were tomorrow's racing form, whilst nervously smoking a cigarette.

I put the completed coffee on the counter before the young man and returned to my paper, so that he wouldn't talk to me either. It didn't work.

"Can I get a bus here?" he asked, producing a stick of gum, which he popped into his mouth and chewed in that slack-jawed way that only rednecks seem to manage.

"No, you have to go out the door," I replied, nodding towards the huge BUS STOP sign through the window.

"Cute," he said, his bravado replacing the nervous, haunted look…unless, of course, it was just the therapeutic nature of my character.

He looked around the room, sighted my other customer, and smiled. She ignored him. She wasn't his type. She had class, or thought she did: After all, she'd paid enough for it. You could tell by the way she wore her mink.

She'd arrived ten minutes before him, also looking shook up. She had asked if there was anywhere from where she could make a phone call, noticing that my payphone had a tattered and dusty 'OUT OF ORDER' notice taped to it.

On finding out that this piece of junk was the only example of Alexander Graham Bell's masterpiece within three miles, she had ordered black coffee, which (judging by the slight slur of her very careful, educated speech, and the faint smell of whiskey), was intended to sober her up. She had carefully carried the coffee to the table where she now sat – (between the Ladies washroom and the very old Wurlitzer jukebox) – and begun to work towards contracting lung-cancer by chain-smoking three cigarettes, lighting each one from the previous butt.

"Is there a bus soon?" It was the hitchhiker.

"In a hurry to get away?" I asked. The nervous look returned. I let it hang for a couple of seconds before glancing back at the clock on the wall. "Last bus is at midnight," I said. "You've got half an hour."

He nodded, not even realising that I was amusing myself with him.

"You okay, buddy?" I asked. "You don't look so good."

"I had an accident a little way back up the road." He gestured back that way with a nod. "Got hit by a car."

My other customer spluttered, mid-swallow, as if her coffee was too hot – you know, the way people always do on TV, but hardly ever do in real life. Unless, of course, if it's a *real* big shock. She wasn't ignoring him now.

"How far back was that?" she asked, unable to stop herself.

"About half a mile," he supplied, studying her. "A big blue Oldsmobile. Knocked me clean across the road. Jeez, I'm lucky to be alive!"

The look of relief on her face made me wonder if I'd have to sponge the seat down. The redneck noticed it too.

"Why, Ma'am, you wouldn't happen to know anything about it, would you?" he asked.

"No, I was just asking," she said, far too hurriedly.

To say that there was a pregnant silence would be an understatement; it was practically going into labour. Just as the waters were about to break, the door rattled open.

My latest customer was a frail looking teenage girl. She had blonde hair that hung straight and long, almost to her waist, and huge brown eyes that pleaded to whomever they fell upon.

They fell upon me, so I stepped from behind the counter.

"Are you alright?" I asked, though the answer was obvious. She shook her head, unable to speak. Her chin began to tremble, and tears were welling up in her eyes.

I sat her at a table near the counter, which contained a chessboard (I occasionally play against the customers); a week old copy of the International Herald Tribune, and a 'STAFF ONLY' notice. When I was sure that she wouldn't fall off her chair because of her quiet but convulsive sobbing, I fixed her a large cappuccino.

The hitchhiker, who had been eyeing the girl quite closely, (too closely for my liking), sauntered away as I put the cappuccino in front of her. Perhaps he was afraid that he might be expected to make himself useful, or maybe he had other business. He stopped beside the classy chain smoker and leered down at her, though she'd retreated back behind her menu and her feigned disinterest.

"Don't worry," I said to the youngster. "You'll be alright here. Drink up." I pushed the cappuccino closer to her.

She glanced up briefly. "I can't afford to pay you," she whispered.

"On the house," I smiled. "You don't have to talk unless you want to, but if you do, I'll listen. I'm here to help."

I sat down, opened up the Herald Tribune and made a show of reading the funnies as nonchalantly as I could. The whole room was stuck in a grotesque and eerily silent freeze-frame that left me feeling it was time to switch on the radio. I got up, did so, then returned to the table, and the funnies.

The tinny little speaker on the transistor radio did no justice to the music coming out of it, but it somehow magically reanimated the room.

The hitchhiker put down his espresso and sat down facing the chain smoker, which kind of forced her to notice him. She stubbed out her cigarette and did not light another. Maybe he thought she looked better smoking, because he produced a packet of Lucky Strikes from his shirt pocket, extracted one with his teeth and shook another half-way out of the packet with a deft flick of the wrist. He extended it towards her.

"Do you smoke Ma'am?" he asked, proving that I had no monopoly on sarcasm. She eyed him levelly, trying to read his face.

"Yes, thank you," she replied, taking it.

He tore a match from its book and lit both cigarettes, starting with hers. No doubt, she was supposed to think that they have real southern gentlemen in whatever trailer park he came from. Perhaps they do, but I somehow doubted that he was one of them.

"It was you, wasn't it?" he asked quietly, though his voice had a brittle edge.

She started to shake her head, but even she realised that any attempt at denial was futile. ""My God, I'm so sorry," she said. Her face began to crease, as if she was going to cry, but she couldn't force the expression any further. She wasn't the crying type and she'd probably never been sorry in her life.

"You could've fucking killed me, lady!" he hissed. He raised his hand, as if he was going to bang it down on the table, but with a great effort, he let it gently fall palm downwards. "You'd have left me there to die rather than let the cops smell the booze on your breath!"

"I'm so sorry," she said again, lamely. "I'll make it up to you, I swear it. I – I can't afford a scandal."

"A scandal?" he repeated. He looked around to see if I was listening, but my eyes were still fixed on the 'Marmaduke' cartoon strip, and I had an amused look on my face.

"Damn' right you'll make it up to me."

"I'll give you a thousand dollars," she said, "as long as you keep quiet about this. If the press got hold of this…"

"The press?" asked the hitchhiker. "Why would they be interested in you?"

"Because I'm Senator Harrison's wife," she announced, flatly. "If my…my habits were to be made public, it would harm his career."

"No shit!" he agreed. "Twenty thousand!"

"What?"

"Twenty thousand, and you drive me to the nearest bank to collect it as soon as you're sober. Drink your coffee!"

"I can't drive you anywhere," she said. "After I… after the accident, my car went off the road and hit a tree. I'm surprised you didn't see the wreck. I was lucky to walk away myself." She stubbed out her cigarette and looked defiantly into his eyes. "I'm catching the bus with you."

"You certainly are, Ma'am," he said, leaning froward.

In the corner of my eye, I saw him reach out beneath the table and rest a hand on her stockinged knee. Her jawline hardened, anger flaring in her eyes and her whole body stiffened, but she didn't pull away. She realised that in addition to her knee, he was holding all the cards.

They sat that way in silence and the transistor radio behind my counter was the only sound. The gruff-voiced late night DJ announced that the last track had been 'Misty' by Earl Garner, which he had played at the request of a mystery caller, before giving out some local news: A storm was coming in from the sea, and the state Police were looking for a man in connection with the murder of an elderly bait shop owner…

"Hey mister!" the hitchhiker called. "Let's have some music! What's wrong with the jukebox?"

I got up and switched the machine on, then turned off the radio before returning to my seat opposite the girl.

Mrs. Harrison got up and stood in the dim light of the Wurlitzer, peering down at the faded title-cards, looking for something she liked. The redneck joined her, placing a hand in the small of her back, which she immediately shrugged off. He chose 'That Old Devil Called Love' by Billie Holliday. They were having a Hell of a night, I thought, as they returned to their table.

The young girl had stopped crying and I noticed that she'd got through most of her cappuccino.

"Do you want another of those?" I asked.

"I don't want to be any trouble," she said timidly.

"It's okay," I said. "We got loads of this stuff. Nobody ever buys it anyway."

She smiled for the first time, a warm, innocent, slightly buck-toothed smile that made me wonder how she'd ever managed to find the ball of misery that she'd carried in. I fixed her another drink and placed it in front of her.

"Thank you," she said quietly, warming her fragile little hands on the cup.

"Feeling better?" I asked, sitting back down.

She nodded. "I'm sorry to have been a trouble."

"You haven't been," I assured her. "Will it help to talk about it?"

"I don't know what to do," she said, and began to lose her composure again. She took a deep breath before continuing: "It's my parents. They're getting a divorce. I heard them talking about it tonight. I'm never going to see my Dad again..." The tears came again.

"Hey, don't cry," I offered, patting her hand briefly. "Of course you'll see him again." I reached back and passed her a paper napkin from the dispenser at the end of the counter behind me. She dabbed her eyes, sniffling quietly.

"I won't see him again," she said at last. "He's moving to New York."

"That's tough," I said sympathetically, "but surely you'll be able to visit."

"I even thought of killing myself," she continued, as if she hadn't heard me. "I took an overdose, but it didn't do anything except make me sick. I thought that if they found me there on the garage floor and realised what they were doing, and how it was making me feel, they might change their minds."

"It doesn't work that way," I said, "believe me. They'd probably blame each other. What did you take?"

"Oh, just the stuff from the medicine cabinet in the bathroom; painkillers and sleeping tablets and stuff. It didn't do anything. I feel okay." She smiled again. "I just got up and started walking until I ended up here." She gave her eyes another dab with the soggy napkin, then looked up at the clock on the wall.

"Is there someplace I can clean up?" she asked. I pointed to the ladies washroom at the back of the diner.

"Be my guest," I said.

She made her way there slowly, careful to avoid the eyes of Mrs. Harrison and my other customer. I saw each of them glance up at the clock, just as she had.

The storm came suddenly, with a crack like cannon fire. The noise was accompanied by a blue flash, which momentarily lit up the sky through the windows. Less than a second later, the rain began to batter my fragile establishment in a merciless onslaught. It was eleven fifty-five.

Mrs. Harrison and the hitchhiker got up and ambled slowly to the door. They looked out, apprehensively, at the storm.

"Don't worry," I said. "The bus always stops here."

The expressions on both of their faces turned to looks of relief. I went behind my counter and poured black coffee into a Styrofoam cup, onto which I clipped a plastic lid.

Right on cue, the bus ground to a halt outside. The door hissed open and the driver disembarked, the peak of his cap pulled low, and the collar of his oilskin coat turned up around his ears. He came bolting into the diner to escape the rain, touching the peak of his cap with a gloved hand as he passed Mrs. Harrison.

"Hi Nick," I said, passing him the coffee I had just made.

"How's it going?" he asked, taking it and dropping the exact change on the counter.

"Fine," I replied. "Got a couple of passengers for you."

He glanced back at them. "You ready to go as you are?" he asked.

The hitchhiker said nothing, turning instead to look at the storm.

"We have no baggage," offered Mrs. Harrison.

"Not the kind you need to open the trunk for, at least," I thought.

"Well, let's get going," said Nick. "Thanks for the coffee."

The three of them went out into the rain and boarded the bus. A couple of seconds later, the girl appeared from the washroom and, seeing the bus, bolted straight outside and climbed aboard herself.

I sighed and resignedly fixed myself an espresso. Before I had chance to take a sip, the young girl burst through the door.

"Please help me," she said. "The driver says he won't let me on without the fare. He says I should catch the one going the other way tomorrow, but I just need to get to a town so I can call my parents. Please, can you lend me the fare? I swear I'll pay you back, I swear it!"

Shrugging, I opened the till, took out a ten-dollar bill and extended it towards her.

"Thank you," she said earnestly, but her expression turned immediately to one of abject despair as the bus pulled away.

"No!" she wailed, running back to the door, but she stopped, realising the futility of the action.

Her spirit suddenly broken, she returned to my 'STAFF ONLY' table and dropped into the chair, crying into her hands.

I returned the ten dollars to the till and fixed a cappuccino. Taking it, along with my espresso, I joined her at the table and watched her, not really sure how I might comfort her.

"How could he just drive off like that?" she sobbed, not bothering to take her hands away from her face.

"He knew that I was coming back to borrow the fare. He's just evil!"

"He's just doing his job," I told her, sliding her drink towards her. "Look, stop crying. I'll make sure you get back to your parents. As soon as my shift's over, I'll get you home."

She looked up, a faint sign of hope on her tear-streaked face. "You will?" she asked. "Oh, thank you!" She grabbed one of my hands in both of hers and gripped it tightly. She even managed a smile as she looked into my eyes.

"It's true what they say," she said. "Cold hands, warm heart."

I gently freed myself from her grip. "Yeah, now drink your cappuccino and cheer up," I ordered with mock severity.

We sat for a while, just listening to the storm outside. She'd relaxed a lot since she first came in and she seemed like a nice kid. She certainly didn't seem to deserve the rough ride she'd had, but I guess we all have our allotted share of misery in life, whether we ask for it or not.

"What's your name?" I asked.

"It's Laura," she replied, "Laura Spenser."

"Well, Laura," I said. "Have you ever played chess?"

"Only a little." She paused, remembering, and a fond smile touched the edges of her mouth as a happy memory toyed with her. "My Grandfather taught me when I was a little girl."

I smiled. She was still a little girl. It's funny, though a little sad when the innocent don't even realise that they're still innocent. It sort of makes you wonder how cynical they'll become when they grow up for real.

"Let's play," I said, opening up the board and setting out the pieces.

"I'm really not very good," she protested.

"Neither am I," I assured her, "and I need the practice. Call it the price of a lift home."

She shrugged. "Okay," she said, "but don't make me look too bad."

"Scout's honour," I promised. "You go first."

She didn't start off too badly. An Indian opening, as it's called, is a reasonably good way to begin, in preparation for clearing your back line, in case you have to castle to get your king out of danger, later in the game. By the sixth move, however, her concentration started slipping. She had failed to dominate the centre of the board, and had left two pieces unprotected. I had no option but to take the exposed knight…

The real challenge that the game presented to me was to avoid clearing all her pieces without looking as though I was patronising her. It required as much planning as any game, even the ones you want to win.

Eventually, and with a lot of hard work, I managed to manoeuvre myself into a position where I could be checkmated. Although she was obviously a beginner, she was a bright kid and saw her chance.

"Well done," I said. "I thought you said you weren't good?"

"Oh, I think you were letting me win," she smiled. As I said, she was a bright kid.

I began to put away the pieces. "I don't suppose you want a rematch?" I asked.

She shook her head, trying politely to stifle a yawn. "No thanks," she said. "I'd rather quit while I'm ahead."

"Get some rest if you can get comfortable," I offered. "I've got one or two chores to do before I close up." I got up and took our empty cups back behind the counter.

"Can I help?" asked Laura.

"No, it's okay," I replied, "it's all automated back here."

She leaned forward over the table, resting her head on her folded arms. Her eyes closed and within seconds her breathing grew slow and deep.

I carried the dirty cups through the narrow swing door behind the counter into the kitchen, to be washed. I have another of those little transistor radios in there and I switched it on as I set about filling the dishwasher.

"…and that was 'Requiem' by Denny Zeitlin," said the late night DJ. "Now it's over to Bob for the local news update at two a.m. What's happening Bob?"

"Well, Gerry, the big story tonight is that the state police have called off their search for the murderer of Sam Green, owner of the Charlesville Bait Shop. It appears that the man who committed this terrible crime has himself become a fatality in a road traffic accident. He was run over and killed on the south road sometime this evening. Unfortunately, the driver of the car, Mrs Ellen Harrison, wife of Senator Harrison, was also killed when she skidded off the road into a tree. We'll have more news for you on that as it comes in…"

Leaving the dishwasher running, I went back out into the diner. The girl had vanished. I smiled as I unplugged the jukebox and reached into the washrooms to switch off the lights. All in all, it had been quite a night…

That's exactly how it all happened, at least, as far as I can remember. If you don't believe me, you could always make the trip to Los Angeles. When you get there, find a young woman called Laura Spenser.

She's studying psychology at UCLA. She splits her vacation time between visiting her mother in San Francisco and her father in Manhattan. At the moment, she's doing a thesis on near death experiences. It was inspired, no doubt, by the one that she'd had some years ago, whilst being taken from the floor of her parent's garage to the local hospital, suffering from a huge overdose of painkillers and sleeping tablets.

Of course, if that's too much trouble, you could always just wait until you get here yourself. It's only a matter of time. It doesn't matter whether you end up catching Nick's bus or the one going the other way; you'll find yourself here. Make sure you bring some change for a coffee in case your mouth gets dry. It sometimes does when you're waiting for the last bus.

Vermin

The mystery and intrigue
Are more than I can bear.
I want to find out where you are
I'll track you to your lair.
I've set a thousand traps for you
That never have been sprung.
I want to see your carcass
Upon my gallows hung.

I'll hunt you down and kill you,
Exterminate your lice,
To be free of their crawling
And the itching of their bites.
When I catch a glimpse of you,
You bare your yellow teeth.
I shudder as I see the litter,
Suckling underneath.

You're the blackest of Hell's creatures,

You'd gladly make your bed,

In filthy, slimy places,

Where angels fear to tread.

At last I've found your hiding place,

But I can't bear the pain.

Oh my God, you've made yourself

At home inside my brain.

If your name's not down, you're not coming in

…So, there I was…dead!

I mean, I didn't expect that! I'd been abseiling down the north face of the Hilton, three feet from Lord Hambleton's window, and the rope had snapped. A half-second later, I caught a glimpse of the necklace as I was flying past. A half second after that, I caught a glimpse of the pavement. The only thing is, the fall was that bad that I ended up staring back at my own burst open face (and it's not a pretty sight).

…And all because I was stupid enough to twist in the air and miss the van. You see, I have this van with mattresses in it, parked in the street below, just in case, like. Only this time, there's a little kid playing on it. Well…if I'd landed on him he'd be dead, wouldn't he? So, like a proper berk, I twisted…and ended up looking like a bloody great jam stain on the pavement.

The next thing I knew, there was Saint Peter, book in one hand, keys in the other, standing at a marble lectern, welcoming me to the hereafter.

Now, this situation might not seem strange to you, but I've never really been what you'd call 'a believer', (if you know what I mean). So, as you can imagine, I was a little bit off guard.

"Name?" he asked.

"Who wants to know?" I says.

"The Lord God Almighty," he announced, all fire-and-brimstone like.

"Are you God, then?" I said, being a bit cocky.

"No," he said, "I'm Saint Peter," (and that's how I knew who he was).

"God wants to know!" he shouted, with a stern frown.

Well, I thought for minute, being the cautious type, then said: "Isn't God supposed to know everything?"

Well, I'd got him there, hadn't I?

Then, of course, he comes out with the old line: "Do not tempt the Lord thy God!"

Well, I'm not tempting anyone, am I? I'm just asking. Jesus, he made the meanest Bow Street Magistrate look like a leftie bloody Social Worker! I told him so and all! Of course, he took it the wrong way and started bellowing something about not getting into Heaven, which was just what I was after. I told him that, and he just stopped dead, flabbergasted.

"What?" he said. "You don't want to get into Heaven? You plan to spend eternity in the fires of Hell? Are you mad?"

"Will that get me into Hell?" I asked.

"Hmm, not since they invented psychiatry and phased out demonic possession," he replied.

"Well," I said, "I'm not mad anyway. Now, if you don't mind, I'd like to get set off, so pull the lever, or push the button, or do whatever you do, but pack me off to eternal damnation."

He shook his head sadly, and you know, for just a second, I actually believe he did feel sad.

"It doesn't work like that, I'm afraid," he said. "If your name is written in this book, you're coming in…whether you like it or not."

Well, that was a bit of a shock. I never thought they might *make* you go there. I mean, they couldn't, could they?

"Well, I'm not *tellin'* yer me bloody name!" I shouted.

"We already know your name. *He* knew your name before you were born!" he replied.

"So why the bleedin' Hell did you ask me in the first place?" I asked, (and to my mind, it's not an unreasonable question).

"It's a formality," he said. "Besides, the responses we get are a good indicator of personalities. It helps us to root out the troublemakers."

"So, what do you do with the troublemakers?" I asked, looking for a legal loophole.

"We forgive them," he said.

Innit bloody marvellous?! I'd been dead for five minutes and it was already going tits up! I decided to change my tactics.

"Your honour," I said, stepping up to the lectern so that he could look down on me, the way the Judge looks down at the Counsel for the defence when he's begging the old git to shave a few months off your sentence. "I've got a good reason for wanting to go down there. Surely you must know of a way I can be sent down there."

He looked up from the book, his finger still resting on the list of names to keep his place. "I don't make the rules," he said, then carried on reading.

I turned around and walked twenty paces away. When I faced him again, he didn't have to look down to see me, just across. It felt a bit more like being in the Dock…and you know what? I felt more comfortable.

"I demand a fair trial," I said. "Do you hear me?"

"Alright," he said at last. "I'm listening."

"Well, it's like this you see," I told him. "I don't want to get into heaven, on account of Doris."

"Doris?" he asked.

"Doris," I confirmed. "My late Missus. I met her fifteen years ago on Berwick Street, saw her a couple of times, and within a month, I wasn't even paying anymore. From the moment we moved in together, we had it made. She was a real cracker was Doris, but she won't be in Heaven – there'd be too many red faces when she recognised old clients."

"I see," said Saint Peter.

"Well, that's about it," I continued. "I don't want to go to Heaven. I'd miss my Doris. Besides, I'm a real bad 'un when it comes down to it."

Saint Peter scratched his head. "I don't think that you truly understand the concept of Hell," he said.

"I don't care," I replied. "You can't make me stay here!"

He looked down at his book again, as if something important was missing. When he looked back up, he'd come over all sorrowful, like.

"Very well," he said. "You are free to choose your own destiny, but I beg you to reconsider."

"Don't talk like a nit!" I said, and a second later, I was in total darkness.

Suddenly, as if from nowhere, there was a huge explosion of flame and black smoke. And there, in the flickering red light in front of me stood Satan himself.

Opening a book with pages made from raw human flesh, he looked down at it, then at me. A gust of his rancid breath swept over me and made me wretch.

"What are you doing here, worm?" he asked, in a suitably booming gasp.

I told him my name and he began rooting through his book. Flecks of fresh blood splashed here and there as he leafed the pages backwards and forwards.

"I don't seem able to find your name," he said.

Taking as deep a breath as I could in the foul stench, I told him what I'd told Saint Peter.

"Ah, Doris!" he said jovially, flicking to a page with one corner folded over, "…and already the writing is changing!"

"What are you on about?" I asked. "When do I get to see my Doris?"

"You don't," chuckled the Devil. "This is Hell, remember? Oh, Doris arrived here straight after she died, as you knew she would. The only thing is, everybody gets just one last chance to change their destiny at the moment of death, just as you did."

"So?" I asked, panic starting to rise up in my gut.

"Well, don't you see? Whilst you, who died saving some child (who will, incidentally, grow up to become one of your country's most ruthless murderers), threw away your chance of salvation by selfishly demanding to come down here so you could have what you want; Doris, the pious cow, genuinely repented all her sins, so I had to send her upstairs…forever…leaving you down here with me…forever!"

www.ingramcontent.com/pod-product-compliance
Lightning Source LLC
Chambersburg PA
CBHW010348220726
48290CB00016B/2678